The Right Number of Elephants

Story by Jeff Sheppard
Pictures by Felicia Bond

HarperTrophy
A Division of HarperCollinsPublishers

The Right Number of Elephants
Text copyright © 1990 by Jeff Sheppard
Illustrations copyright © 1990 by Felicia Bond
Printed in the U.S.A. All rights reserved.

Library of Congress Cataloging-in-Publication Data
Sheppard, Jeff.
  The right number of elephants.
  Summary: A counting book in which a little girl
relies on the help of some eager elephants.
  [1. Elephants—Fiction. 2. Counting.] I. Bond,
Felicia, ill.   II. Title.
PZ7.S54395Ri 1990   [E]   90-4148
ISBN 0-06-025615-X
ISBN 0-06-025616-8 (lib. bdg.)
ISBN 0-06-443299-8 (pbk.)

First Harper Trophy edition, 1992.

For A'yen Tran

J.S.

For my buddy, Julia

F.B.

I f you suddenly need to pull a train
out of a tunnel
and save everyone on board,
then the right number of elephants is

10

But if you just mean to paint the ceiling
and there isn't a ladder to be found,
then the right number of elephants is

9

And when you go to the beach
with all your friends
on a very warm day

and you simply must have shade,
then the right number of elephants is

But if the sky grows very dark
and it suddenly starts to rain
(with lightning and thunder as well),
then the right number of elephants is

And if you'd like a bit of company
on a very deserted street
at a very deserted time of day,
then the right number of elephants is

Of course, if you just want to impress
the neighbors with a quick circus,
then the right number of elephants is

And if you're challenged to a race
by a particularly unpleasant person,
then the right number of elephants is

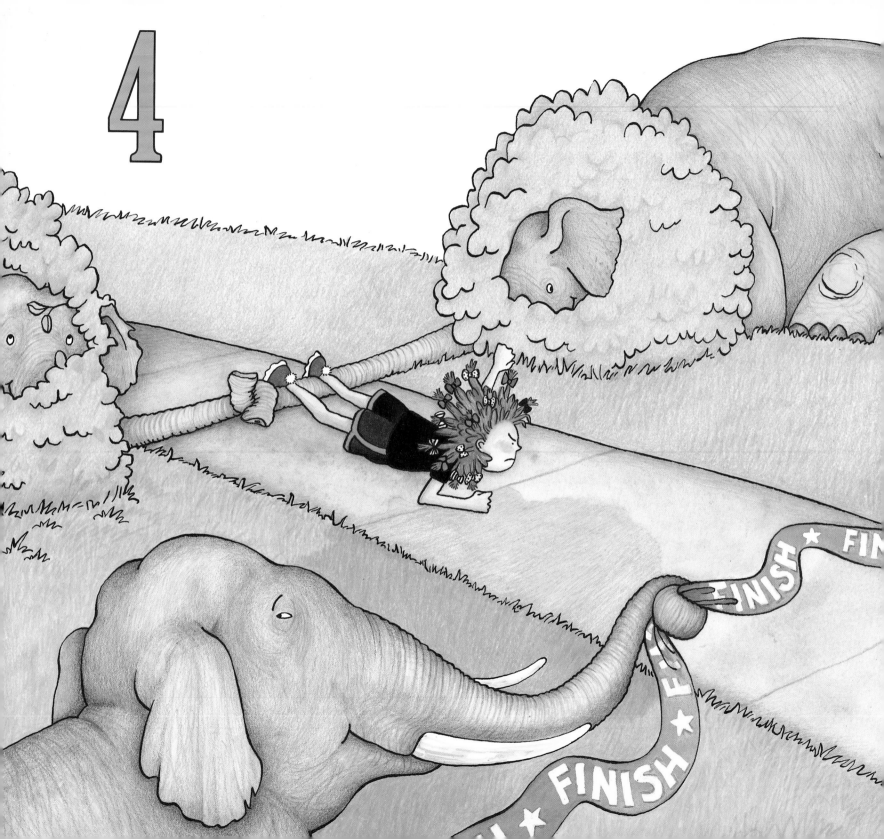

But if it's just a fast game of cards you want,
then the right number of elephants is

And if you need a swing to amuse
your little brother
so you can do important things,

then the right number of elephants is **2**

But when you need
a very special friend

for a very special moment,

then the right number of elephants is